THERE'S A
DRAGON
IN MY
STOCKING!

For Charlotte – T.N.

For my wonderful Primary School – Harper
Hill Primary School, Buxton, Derbyshire –
S.H.

STRIPES PUBLISHING
An imprint of the Little Tiger Group
1 Coda Studios, 189 Munster Road,
London SW6 6AW

A paperback original
First published in Great Britain in 2017

Text copyright © Tom Nicoll, 2017
Illustrations copyright © Sarah Horne, 2017
Author photograph © Kaye Nicoll, 2017

ISBN: 978-1-84715-884-0

A CIP catalogue record for this book is available
from the British Library.

Printed and bound in the UK.

10 9 8 7 6 5 4 3 2 1

THERE'S A DRAGON IN MY STOCKING!

TOM NICOLL

ILLUSTRATED BY
SARAH HORNE

stripes

CHAPTER 1

(NOT SO) SILENT NIGHT

'Twas the night before Christmas, when all through the house,

Not a creature was stirring, not even a Mini-Dragon.

"ERIC, WAKE UP!"

So maybe it wasn't quite true about the Mini-Dragon. He was definitely stirring.

"Pan, what's wrong?" I moaned, sitting up in bed and switching on my lamp.

"Someone's downstairs," said Pan excitedly, from up on my bookshelf.

"Probably just Mum or Dad." I shrugged.

"Seriously, Eric," Pan said. "It's the middle of the night. There's only one person who'd be downstairs at a time like this."

I checked my bedside clock. It was almost four.

"You mean a burglar?" I yawned.

Pan slapped his forehead. "No, not a burglar. I meant there's only one person who'd be downstairs in the middle of night ... on Christmas Eve."

I sat up straight, the penny finally dropping. "No way," I said.

"Well, I can't think of any other possible explanation, can you?" asked Pan.

I couldn't ... but then, I *was* still half asleep. "I don't hear anything," I said.

"I do," said Pan. "Mini-Dragons have excellent hearing. There's a knocking sound and it's definitely coming from the living room. In all those stories you've been telling me, that's where he always goes. Let's go down and meet him!"

Pan had been super-excited to experience his first human Christmas. Mini-Dragons celebrate Christmas, too, but from what Pan had told me, it's a little different. They still give each other gifts but Santa doesn't visit Mini-Dragons. Pan was more than a bit miffed when he realized how many presents he had missed out on over the years. If it really was Santa in our living room, he was going to have a lot of explaining to do.

But the last thing I wanted was to be caught out of bed by my parents. Every year Dad would tell the story about getting up early one Christmas to sneak a peek at his presents only to be caught by my grandad and sent back to bed. Then, when he got up in the morning, Grandad had hidden every one of his presents. I didn't fancy spending all day searching for gifts like Dad had done.

On the other hand, what if it was ... *him*?

"Come on," I said, slipping on my dressing gown and putting Pan into the pocket. I opened my bedroom door and checked for signs of Mum and Dad. The coast was clear. I moved silently along the landing and tiptoed down the stairs.

We were almost at the bottom when I heard it – a faint knocking.

I crept over to the living-room door and pressed my ear up against it. The knocking had stopped but now there was something else.

"Can you hear talking?" whispered Pan.

I nodded. The noise was too muffled to pick out any words but it definitely sounded like someone speaking.

"Can you hear what they're saying?" I asked Pan.

"Not really… Something about going the wrong way…" said Pan.

I took a deep breath, turned the handle and slowly opened the door.

"Wow! Look at all those—" said Pan, before I quickly clamped a hand over his mouth to keep him quiet.

I put Pan down and went to switch on

the main light. But before I got the chance the Mini-Dragon dashed over and turned on the Christmas-tree lights.

I gasped. Above the mantelpiece hung five red stockings embroidered with our names – Mum, Dad, Eric, Posy and Pusskin. Each was overflowing with parcels. But that was nothing compared to the huge pile of presents almost completely obscuring our Christmas tree.

Pan let out a whistle. "You must have been really good this year," he said, pointing at my stocking.

I wasn't so sure about that. In the past year, I had been at least partly responsible for:

- My horrible neighbour Toby being shot into a tree on a rocket-powered scooter.
- Driving a stolen golf buggy through rush-hour traffic.
- Flushing Pan's aunt and uncle down the toilet.

- Convincing half the country that a monster lived beneath the waters of Lake Cress.
- Nearly causing a riot in a cinema.

On the other hand, Pan had definitely played a big part, too. And I had actually done some pretty good things this year. I had:

- Taken in Pan and looked after him.
- Rescued Pan after various dragon-nappings.
- Helped train Pan to fly ... sort of (his takeoffs and landings still need work).

If that's not enough to make Santa's Nice List, then I don't know what is.

As tempting as it was to tear into all the presents, we were downstairs for a reason. Aside from our cat Pusskin, who was curled up asleep on the rug, there was no one else in the room.

"Where is he, then?" I said, looking around.

"I don't know," said Pan, sounding disappointed. "Maybe we just missed him? I can't hear anything now."

"Yeah, maybe..." I said, beginning to wonder if we'd imagined it. "Well, we'd better get back upstairs before Mum and Dad hear us."

I was just about to switch off the tree lights when we heard it again. Talking. It was coming from the old boarded-up fireplace.

"You said this was how we'd get in,"

said the first voice.

"I thought it was…" said the second. "Didn't you see all those pictures of that jolly-looking man in red with the beard on the way over?"

"I think he might be a special case, dear," the first voice sighed.

The voices were muffled but there was something very familiar about them. I exchanged glances with Pan.

"It … almost sounds like…" said Pan, staring fixedly at the fireplace. "But it can't be…"

"There's only one thing for it," said the second voice. "Stand back."

There was silence after that. For a second I thought whoever it was had gone, until I noticed a small circular patch at the foot of the fireplace, glowing redder and redder.

"Wha—" I said, before being cut off by

a blast of flame shooting through the board.
I jumped in fright, stumbling backwards and
almost treading on Pusskin. She let out a
huge hiss and darted off.

I got to my feet just in time to see two tiny winged creatures stepping through the hole that had just appeared in the fireplace, each carrying a rucksack almost the same size as they were. Even with all the soot on their faces, I recognized them at once.

"MUM! DAD!" cried Pan.

CHAPTER 2
LET IT SNOW

"PAN!" the dragons shouted back, rushing towards him. "MERRY CHRISTMAS!"

"What are you guys doing here?" asked Pan. I had never seen him look so happy, or so shocked. I knew the feeling. Well, the shocked part anyway.

"We couldn't miss spending Christmas with our only son," said Pan's mum, Isabel. She looked a lot like Pan but with long curled eyelashes and red-painted claws.

"You never said you were coming," said Pan. Pan regularly borrowed our laptop to speak to his parents and he was right, they hadn't mentioned it once. I'd definitely remember something like that.

"We wanted it to be a surprise," said Pan's dad, Cheng, who also resembled his son, except for his wispy white beard and miniature spectacles.

"It definitely is a surprise," I agreed.

"Eric!" said Pan's parents, flying over to give me a hug. Well, my ankle at least.

"Good to see you," said Cheng. "You're much bigger in real life, you know."

"Er ... thanks," I said. "So, you guys flew here all the way from China?"

A mischievous smile appeared on Mr Long's face. It reminded me of Pan when he was up to no good.

"Actually, we caught a lift," said Cheng. "Flight CH945 – Beijing to London."

"You came in a plane?" asked Pan, looking impressed.

"More like 'on' a plane," said Isabel. "We were on the underside of one of the wings."

"The wings?" I repeated. "How did you stay on?"

"With our claws, of course," said Cheng, waving them at me. "Mini-Dragons are

19

excellent at attaching themselves to aircraft. It's a lovely way to travel."

"Well, it was until you decided to go for a wander just before we landed," said Pan's mum. "Some of the passengers spotted him so we had to get off a few minutes early. We flew the rest of the way. Luckily, you're not too far from the airport."

"You were seen?" gasped Pan.

Cheng waved him away. "They probably just thought they saw some birds or something. Your mother worries too much."

"I do not," Isabel said, raising her voice. "I worry just the right amount."

"Shh!" I said, "You'll wake up my—"

There was a loud thud from upstairs.

Then an "Ouch!"

And then the sound of footsteps coming down the stairs.

"That's my parents," I said, panicking. "You've got to hide."

"We have to *what*?" said Isabel.

"We've been over this, Mum," said Pan. "Eric's parents don't know about Mini-Dragons."

"Still?" said Pan's dad, turning to me. "You mean you've managed to keep Pan hidden all this time?"

"That's right," I said, desperately scanning the room for somewhere to put them.

"That's quite impressive," said Cheng. "Pan's never exactly been one for staying out of trouble. Have you, son?"

Pan frowned. "Me? You just burned a hole through Eric's fireplace!"

I groaned. There wasn't time to try to cover it up. It did kind of look like a little mousehole. So if Mum or Dad spotted it, that would be my story.

"Just keep quiet," I said, scooping up the three Mini-Dragons and cramming them into my stocking, just as the door burst open.

"Eric!" said Mum, in a disappointed voice. "What are you doing up?"

"I ... I ... thought I heard Santa," I said, which was true.

"Did I ever tell you about the time I got
out of bed early on Christmas morning?"
said Dad.

"Yes, Dad, only every Christmas." I
sighed.

"Oh," said Dad. "Well, I think we should

probably go back upstairs. It's really early..."

"PRESENTS!" screamed Posy, my three-year-old sister, bursting into the room and making a beeline towards the tree. She

dived at the pile of presents and ripped open a bright purple box to reveal a men's electric shaving kit.

"Or we could just stay up," yawned Dad.

A couple of hours later our living room was a jumble of wrapping paper and empty boxes. Posy was using her tea set from Santa to entertain an assortment of dolls and teddies. Mum was engrossed in a yoga book I had bought her. Dad was admiring his football boots and Pusskin was batting at a rubber mouse. Meanwhile I was admiring my brand-new electric scooter.

"I know you wanted another Thunderbolt," said Mum, "but after what happened with your first one, we thought it was safer to go for another brand."

"Are you kidding?" I said. "Fireflies are awesome. I can't wait to see what it can do."

"I think you're going to have to," said Dad, parting the curtains and looking out. He pulled them back to reveal our street covered in a white blanket.

"Snow!" shouted Posy.

"A white Christmas," said Mum. "How lovely!"

As much as I wanted to try out my Firefly, it was hard to be too disappointed. Snow! On Christmas Day!

"Hey, we're not finished yet," said Mum, noticing my stocking and going over to pick it up.

My face turned the same colour as the

snow. In the excitement of opening presents, I had forgotten the three Mini-Dragons. They had been keeping surprisingly quiet, which in my experience of Mini-Dragons was very unusual.

"Er … actually, maybe we should leave those ones," I said.

Mum and Dad looked at me like they thought I was coming down with something.

"Eric? Not wanting to open presents?" said Dad. "That's something I never thought I'd hear."

"No… I mean… I just thought it would be nice to have something to open later," I said.

"Your grandparents are coming over, remember," said Mum. "I'm sure they'll bring you something. Here you go, Eric."

Before I could utter another word, she reached inside the stocking and pulled out a green…

…package. I breathed a sigh of relief as I took the parcel from her. I opened it to find a Slugwoman electric toothbrush.

"Thanks," I said, adding it to my pile. "I guess I should go and get dressed now."

"Good idea," said Mum. "I'll get started on the breakfast. Full English, everyone?"

"Yum," I said, grabbing my stocking when no one was looking and heading out of the room.

"Maya?" said Dad as I closed the door. "Has there always been a hole in the fireplace?"

I didn't hang around to hear the rest of the conversation. I raced up the stairs to my room and slammed the door behind me.

"All right, you can come out now," I said, tipping the contents of my stocking out on to my bed. There were toys, sweets, an apple and a satsuma. No Mini-Dragons.

CHAPTER 3

HOME FOR CHRISTMAS

This was a new record. I was used to losing one Mini-Dragon, but three? And before breakfast.

Trying to ignore the sinking feeling in the pit of my stomach, I opened my bedroom door to head back downstairs.

And there they were, coming out of Posy's room.

"And last but not least," said Pan, leading his parents on to the landing, "we have Eric's bedroom, where I've been staying."

"Ah yes, home of the infamous sock

drawer," said Pan's mum dryly.

I swiftly scooped up the three of them and bundled them into my room.

The Mini-Dragons seemed bemused by this. "Everything OK?" asked Pan.

"Of course not," I said. "You were supposed to stay inside the stocking. What have you been up to?"

"Oh, we slipped out ages ago," said Pan. "Don't worry, your parents were too busy trying to assemble Posy's Magic Castle toy. Which looks great, by the way. Just my size…"

"Pan's been giving us a tour," said Isabel.

"He even showed us the actual toilet you flushed his aunt and uncle down," said Cheng, giving me a massive grin. "Couldn't have happened to two more deserving Mini-Dragons."

I couldn't help but smile, too. "All right," I said. "But look, I need you to stay in my room for the rest of the day. My grandparents are coming for Christmas dinner so the house is going to be busier than normal. There's too much risk of you guys being seen."

Mr and Mrs Longs' faces fell.

"You mean I've come all this way and I'm not even going to get to meet your mum?" asked Mrs Long. Mum taught yoga classes over the Internet and Isabel was probably her biggest fan. I'd even had to post her a signed photograph.

"I'm sorry, no," I said.

"I'd hoped we'd at least get to meet Min and Jayden," said Mr Long.

"You couldn't, anyway," said Pan. "They've both gone away for the holidays."

This was true. Jayden was off to France and Min...

Pan and I laughed. "Min's gone to China," said Pan.

"Like dragons passing in the night," chuckled Cheng.

"On the plus side," said Pan, "Toby from next door is away as well. Where's he gone again, Eric?"

"New York." I sighed. All I had heard from Toby for the past month was how amazing his Christmas was going to be. I turned my attention back to the matter at hand. "So you'll stay in my room?"

Pan's mum rolled her eyes but nodded.

"Thanks," I said. "Right ... er ... I don't suppose you could all look that way." I pointed behind them.

Isabel put her hands on her hips. "It's bad enough that you want us to spend all day cooped up in here," she moaned, "but now we have to spend it staring at a wall?"

"Um … no," I said quietly. "I just meant for a minute, while I get dressed."

Her face turned bright red. "Oh. Yes, of course."

Just as I finished getting changed, Mum shouted that breakfast was ready. But in all the chaos, I realized I had forgotten something.

"Pan, we haven't given each other presents yet," I said.

"Ooh, yes, let's exchange gifts," said Pan's mum. "We've got something for both of you."

To my surprise, Pan didn't look very keen. "Er … no…" he said. "Mini-Dragons wait until after dinner."

Pan's dad frowned. "Yes … most do. But you're normally too impatient for that."

"Um … yeah, I'm much more grown up now," said Pan.

"Suit yourself," said Isabel.

"All right," I said, not really sure what was going on. "Later then. Anyway, I'd better go." I was about to head back downstairs when Pan pulled me aside.

"Eric," he whispered. "I need your help."

"What is it?" I asked.

"I haven't got my parents anything," he began. "I wasn't exactly expecting them."

"You and me both," I said.

"I can't think of anything to give them."

It was an interesting problem. I had struggled to figure out what to buy a Mini-Dragon for Christmas but Mini-Dragon parents? I had no idea either. "Leave it with me," I said. "I'll try and think of something."

"Thanks, Eric."

I hurried down to join my family in the kitchen for our traditional Christmas morning fry-up. I could tell by the smell of bacon, sausages and eggs that it wasn't going to disappoint.

"Looks great," said Dad as he came through from the living room. "Guess what—"

Before he could finish, Mum cut him off. "Eric, you're never going to believe it," she said excitedly. "Your friend is coming for dinner!"

Dad looked a bit deflated. "How did you…? I was going to tell him."

Mum looked confused. "Tell him? How did you know?"

"I just got off the phone—" he said.

"*You* just got off the phone?" interrupted Mum. "But I was just speaking to them…"

I couldn't take much more of this. "Who's coming for dinner?" I asked.

"Min!" said Mum.

"Jayden!" said Dad.

There was silence as Mum and Dad stared at each other.

"They're both coming?" I said, grinning.

Mum and Dad nodded. "Min's flight got cancelled," explained Mum. "And since they haven't got anything in for dinner, Min's mum asked if we had room for three more."

"Same for Jayden and his family," said Dad. "The entire airport is shut down, apparently. I guess we could phone back and cancel…"

"Of course we can't," said Mum. "Turn people away at Christmas?"

"Right," said Dad, stroking his beard. "Well, that's twelve I'll be cooking for. Should be fine, I suppose. We do normally end up eating turkey for days afterwards, anyway."

"Yes!" I said. I couldn't believe I'd get to spend Christmas with my friends *and* not have to eat turkey sandwiches every day for the next week. Tucking into my breakfast, I tried not to think too hard about the Mini-Dragons upstairs and all the extra people I had to keep them hidden from. As long as they stayed in my room, everything should be OK.

After breakfast I helped Mum clear up while Dad started on the Christmas dinner.

"Better get the turkey on," said Dad. "Glad I did all the preparation last night. This is the year, Maya."

"You say that every Christmas," sighed Mum.

"But this year I'm definitely going to cook a Christmas dinner that my dad won't be able to find fault with," he said. "I've been researching and planning for months.

This year I'm finally going to serve – THE ULTIMATE CHRISTMAS DINNER."

"I can't wait," said Mum, with an encouraging smile.

I left my parents to it and headed back upstairs. I was relieved to find that all three Mini-Dragons were still there. Pan was showing his parents our copy of the *Encyclopaedia Dragonica*. It was open on a page about Mini-Dragon Christmases. I took a look:

Christmas

Mini-Dragons are huge fans of Christmas, especially the bit about exchanging presents. Traditional dragon gifts include:

Gold

Jewels

Goats

Gift vouchers

Dirty washing selection boxes

I was about to read some more when I froze.

DIIIIIIIING-DONGGGGGG!

"Oh no," I whispered. A horrible thought had occurred to me.

"What's a Ding-Dong?" asked Mrs Long.

I didn't answer. Instead I rushed back downstairs. Mum and Dad were standing in the hall, looking just as horrified as I was.

"No," I said. "Please no."

"It … it … might be Jayden," said Dad. "Or Min…"

It could be… Or it could just be my grandparents. But I couldn't shake the terrible feeling that it wasn't. And it was obvious my parents felt the same.

"You did say the entire airport was shut down," said Mum. "That means…"

Dad walked slowly towards the door and opened it.

It was just as we'd feared.

"Monty!" bellowed Frank Bloom. "They only went and cancelled our flight! Looks like we're going to have to spend Christmas with you."

CHAPTER 4

DING DONG
MERRILY ON HIGH

"Well, aren't you going to invite us in?" said Mr Bloom. "It's freezing out here."

"Oh, of course, come in," said Dad.

While it was no longer snowing, I couldn't get over how much had already fallen. It must have been at least half a metre deep. Even so, it was hard to believe that Toby and his dad could be cold in their matching sheepskin coats. And if Mrs Bloom was cold, she didn't show any sign of it as she tapped away furiously on her phone.

Mr Bloom headed straight into the living room and slumped down on our sofa.

"Absolute disgrace, that airport," he said. "I'll be speaking to my lawyers about this."

"It's not the airport's fault it snowed, Frank," said Mum. "No one was expecting so much to fall so quickly."

Mr Bloom let out an exaggerated laugh. "Snow? Is that why you think they're closed?"

"Well, that's what Eric's friends' parents told us," said Mum. "Speaking of which—"

"Yes, that's what they're *telling* the public," interrupted Mr Bloom, giving the side of his nose a little tap. "But I happen to know a few of the pilots personally and the truth is it has nothing to do with the snow."

"So what happened, then?" asked Dad.

"Gremlins," said Mr Bloom matter-of-factly.

"Gremlins?" I repeated.

Mr Bloom nodded. "Little green creatures… Apparently, some of the passengers on a flight last night claim to have seen one walking along the plane's wing. A couple of the cabin crew and a co-pilot claim they saw it, too. Nutters the lot of them, obviously, but that seems to be enough these days to shut down an airport, trigger a full-scale investigation and completely ruin our Christmas!"

My mouth had suddenly gone very dry. I knew exactly which flight they were talking about.

"Oh, I am sorry," said Mum. "That's awful. But, er ... so Eric's friends—"

"It's so good of you to take us in," Mr Bloom interrupted again. "Obviously we'd rather be in the Big Apple but Toby was so excited when I told him he'd get to spend Christmas with his best friend."

"Who? Oh, you mean Eric," said Dad.

Toby, who had been uncharacteristically quiet up till now, didn't look very happy. In fact, he looked like he was about to cry. "This is the worst Christmas ever," he muttered. "Not a single present."

"Now, Toby," said Mr Bloom. "You do have presents. But we had them sent to the hotel, didn't we?"

"Yeah, but what about the ones from

Santa?" he yelled. "I asked him for dragon toys like the one Eric has."

"I hope he had better luck finding them than we did," said Mr Bloom, throwing a slightly resentful glance in my direction. "Now don't worry, Toby. He'll have delivered them there, too," he continued. "Santa's a busy man – you can hardly expect him to be checking for flight delays. And they're saying the airport will reopen tomorrow, so you'll only have to wait till then."

This didn't seem to console Toby, who threw himself into his mum's arms.

"And Margery's excited, too," continued Mr Bloom, trying his best to ignore his blubbing son. "Didn't stop talking all the way back from the airport about how good it would be to spend Christmas with her favourite neighbours. Right, Margery?"

There was an awkward silence as

everyone looked at Mrs Bloom, who was patting Toby on the back with one hand and swiping her phone with the other. Eventually she looked up, gave a little nod and returned to her messages.

I could see Mum and Dad staring at each other. They were having one of those silent conversations they sometimes have. Usually these are so I wouldn't know what's going on but I was getting quite good at translating them. This was what I could pick up:

Mum: We can't let them stay, we've already got a full house.

Dad: I know... But who's going to be the one to kick them out?

Mum: He's your friend...

Dad: He's not!

Mum: He seems to think he is.

Dad: Well, he's not.

Mum: I'm not telling them.

Dad:	Neither am I.
Mum:	So I guess they're staying then.
Dad:	I guess…
Mum:	Did you tidy away all the

pumpkins?

OK, so I might have misread that last bit.

"Of course you're welcome to stay," said Dad.

"Brilliant!" shouted Mr Bloom as Toby's wails got even louder. Frank put his feet on the coffee table and switched on the TV. "Ah, Christmas telly, you can't beat it. Oh that's right, I forgot how rubbish your TV is compared to ours. That's a shame, the Queen's meant to be doing her speech in 3D this year… Never mind. What time's dinner, Monty?"

"Er…" began Dad, but he was cut off as a familiar sound rang out.

DIIIIIIIIING-DONGGGGGG!

Before anyone had even got up, we could hear the front door open and seconds later a tall, grey-haired man bounded into the room, dressed like he had just come from climbing Mount Everest. A smaller, rather weary-looking woman trailed after him.

"MERRY CHRISTMAS!" bellowed the old man.

"Merry Christmas, Grandad!" I said, throwing my arms round him.

"Oh, Eric, you get bigger every time I see you," said my gran, barging her husband out of the way and squeezing me tight. "You'll be the size of your grandad soon – though hopefully not as big a pain." She whispered this last part, giving me a wink. Then she shoved a parcel into my arms. "Here you go!"

"Thanks, Gran," I said, tearing open the paper. Of course I knew what it was. A hand-knitted jumper, same as ever. The quality varied from year to year. Some years they were all right. Others they were beyond horrible. This year she had gone for green with a picture of...

"A dragon!" I said, breaking into a smile. "Thanks, I love it."

The rest of my family got jumpers, too. Posy's had a snowman on it, Dad's had a football and Mum had what was meant to be a person doing a yoga pose.

"Your mum told us that you've been mad about dragons lately," said Gran. "So I thought... George, what are you doing?"

As I slipped the jumper on over my shirt, I saw Grandad in the corner of the room, half hidden by our tree. "Just checking out their decorations," he replied. "Same tree again, eh, Monty? We upgraded ours – went with the SuperFir 3000. *Which Christmas Tree?* magazine voted it best tree on the market."

At that, Toby looked up, rubbing his eyes. "Yeah, last year," he said, a trace of that familiar Toby smirk beginning to appear as he peeled himself out of his mum's arms. "This year everyone knows that no tree beats the Evergreen X-MA5."

Grandad's mouth opened and closed a few times but nothing came out. Gran and

Dad were struggling not to laugh.

"Who are these people?" asked Grandad, a little bluntly.

"These are our neighbours," said Mum. "They're going to be joining us for dinner."

Mr Bloom stood up and extended his hand to Grandad. "Monty Bloom. Pleasure to meet you."

"Course it is," said Grandad. "Ha, just kidding, good to meet you… Say, you wouldn't be the same Bloom that beat my son in a camping competition?"

"Sure would," said Mr Bloom. "And I've got the tooth mark in my bum to prove it. Want to see?"

"Er… No, that's OK," muttered Grandad, backing off a little. "Anyway, why's he looking so miserable?" he said, pointing at Toby. "Has no one told him it's Christmas?"

Mum quickly filled Grandad in on why the Blooms were here.

"Best thing that's happened to you all year," declared Grandad. "Nothing beats Christmas with the Crisps. I mean, you will have to put up with my son's cooking…"

Mr Bloom and Toby gave a little chuckle, much to the annoyance of my dad.

"But on the plus side," continued Grandad, "we play tons of games. Sometimes I even let other people win. What do you say? Who's up for a game of Moneyopoly?"

"What's Moneyopoly?" asked Toby.

Grandad looked at Toby as if he had just asked what Christmas was. "You've never played Moneyopoly? Don't you play games?"

"Yeah, I play games," said Toby. "All the time. But I've never heard of that one. Is it one of those olden-times games that comes on cartridges instead of discs?"

"It comes on a board," Grandad said. "You roll the dice. You have little pieces you move around. You buy streets and hotels and you get money for winning beauty contests."

Toby leaned over to his dad. "What's he talking about?" he whispered.

Frank let out a huge laugh but, before he could answer, he was cut off by that familiar sound.

DIIIIIIIIIING-DONGGGGGG!

CHAPTER 5
PEACE ON EARTH

With the arrival of Jayden and Min's families, our living room was more than a little cramped. Mum had quickly armed everyone with a mince pie and a sherry (fizzy drinks for the kids). Posy, meanwhile, was enjoying serving everyone imaginary drinks from her new tea set.

I was trying to finish my lemonade as quickly as I could so I could take Jayden and Min to meet our *other* house guests.

"It's so nice of you to have us all," said Jayden's mum.

"Not a problem, Laila," said Dad.

"Bit snug though, isn't it?" said Min's dad. "Maybe us three should go back to the restaurant."

"Don't be silly, Han," said Mum. "I mean, it'll be a bit of a squeeze for dinner, but it'll be fine."

"That's a lot of people to cook for, son," said Grandad. "You want me to take over? I used to cook for three hundred men every night in the army."

Gran rolled her eyes. "That figure goes up every year," she muttered.

"No, thank you," said Dad, through gritted teeth. "I'll manage."

"Right you are," said Grandad, sounding doubtful. "More people means more money for me in Moneyopoly!" He went over to our toy chest and lifted out a box. "Who's up for a game?"

Toby shot up his hand. Min and Jayden were about to raise theirs, too, when I grabbed them and quickly led them out of the room. "Come with me," I said.

"Hang on," said Min. "We'll get your presents."

"Er… No, leave them," I said. "Pan wants to open them later. I've got something to show you, though."

"Is it your new scooter?" asked Jayden as we slipped up the stairs. "Cos I already know about that. Your mum asked me which one to get. You've no idea how hard it was to keep it a surprise."

"Thanks, I love it. But it's not about my scooter," I said, opening my bedroom door to reveal three Mini-Dragons perched on the windowsill, looking out at the back garden. I breathed a sigh of relief that they were actually still in my room where I'd left them.

Min let out an excited squeal, before
quickly clamping her hands over her mouth.
"Mrs Long, Mr Long," said Jayden,
rushing over to greet them.

"When did you get here? *How* did you get here?" said Min.

As Pan's parents retold the story of their trip, it was clear from the looks they were giving me that Min and Jayden had both realized that the reason they weren't away on holiday was because of our Mini-Dragon visitors. Of course Mr Bloom had told them his gremlin theory, too.

"What are you doing up there?" I asked Pan's parents, changing the subject.

Mrs Long let out a sigh. "What, so now we can't even look out of the window?"

"Er … no," I said quietly. "I was just wondering what you were looking at."

"Oh," she replied, sounding slightly sheepish. "We were just looking at all the snow. I'm sorry, dear, I didn't mean to snap. I think it's being cooped up inside that's doing it."

"You only just got here," I said.

"The three of us were talking about how nice it would be to get out there," said Pan's dad. "It reminds me of the snow we get in the mountains back home. Right, Pan?"

"Yeah," agreed Pan. "Except you guys never let me go out in it."

"That's because you used to make too much noise and set off avalanches," said his mum.

Pan gazed outside longingly. "Well, there's not much chance of that happening here."

"Let's do it," said Jayden. "We can build snowdragons."

All three Mini-Dragons' faces lit up.

"I don't know..." I said. "It's a bit risky. We'd have to get them downstairs and then someone might see them."

I looked to Min. She was normally the most sensible of all of us, so I was sure she'd agree with me.

"Actually," she said, "Pan's parents can fly out of the window. And Pan can sort of fly now, too, so they could just give him a hand with his landing, couldn't they? And there's so much snow, they could easily hide if anyone comes out."

Everyone stared at me hopefully.

What was I going to say? It was Christmas, after all.

"I'll get my wellies," I said.

I had to admit, bringing the dragons outside was a great idea. First we built a little snow wall to conceal the parts of the garden visible from the kitchen window. Then we spent the next hour:

- Building snowmen.
- Building snowdragons.
  (We used old gardening
  gloves for wings and
  twigs for claws.)

- Making snow angels.
  (The Mini-Dragons
  had the advantage
  here with their
  wings.)

- Building Mini-
  Dragon igloos.
  (These didn't take
  very long.)

And, of course:

- Having snowball
  fights.

As it turns out, Mini-Dragons are excellent at these. Well, maybe not the throwing part – their snowballs are tiny. But being so quick and small, they're virtually impossible to hit. And even if you do happen to come close, they can just melt the snow in mid-air with their fire breath.

Min, Jayden and I were just about to call it a draw with Pan and his parents when three large snowballs whacked us in the back of our heads.

"OWWWWW!" the three of us cried.

"Ha ha!" cackled a voice from behind. It was Grandad. "Bullseye!" he shouted.

"Quick, hide," I whispered. But the Mini-Dragons didn't need me to tell them, diving inside their tiny igloos.

Rubbing the back of my head, I turned round to see Grandad, closely followed by a grinning Toby and his dad.

"You should have told us you wanted a snowball fight," said Grandad, pulling down his snow goggles.

"You were busy with your game," I said.

"We're done now," said Grandad. "I cleaned up, as usual. In fact, the only reason I was able to convince these two to come out was because they owed me so much money. Anyway, what do you say, three versus three? Sound fair? Three, two, one – fire!"

I was just about to say no when a snowball whacked me on the shoulder, knocking me to the ground.

"Eric!" shouted Min.

"Run," I said. "Run for your lives!"

I realize that might sound a bit dramatic but I knew that Grandad took his snowball fights very seriously.

As I scrambled to my feet, Min dived behind a rose bush and Jayden found cover behind some compost bags. This left me alone and vulnerable.

"Take no prisoners," yelled Grandad.

I doubted very much that the Blooms had been planning to, as they began pelting snowballs in my direction.

I narrowly dodged Toby's first shot, then ducked out of the way of Mr Bloom's, grabbing a handful of snow while I was at it. But before I could even pack it into a ball, a third snowball, hurled with precision aim by my grandad, knocked the snow out of my hand and into my face.

The Blooms and Grandad were in hysterics as they grabbed more snow. The three of them were lining up to get me when suddenly Min and Jayden came storming out from their shelter. As they ran a barrage of

snowballs left their hands, sailing towards
Grandad.

He jumped over one.

He ducked under another.

He twirled past a third.

He sidestepped
a fourth, yawning
theatrically as he
did so.
   Then, incredibly, he
actually caught the fifth
and the sixth and, before
anyone could blink, had returned them to
their owners, almost knocking Min and
Jayden over.

"This is hopeless," I cried as we retreated behind the shed.

"Your grandad moves like a ninja," noted Min. "It's impossible to hit him."

"Psst," came a voice at our feet. We glanced down to see three annoyed-looking Mini-Dragons.

"Pan, what are you doing here?" I whispered. "You're supposed to be hiding in your igloos."

"Yeah, mate, this is no place for a Mini-Dragon," said Jayden.

"If we'd stayed in our igloos we'd have been trampled on by those barbarians," said Mrs Long.

"We want to help," said Pan.

"No offence, Pan," said Min, "but even between the three of you, you wouldn't be able to throw a snowball hard enough to hit them."

The Mini-Dragons didn't seem to be put off by this. In fact, they started grinning.

"Oh, we're not going to throw any snowballs," said Pan's mum.

"Then how are you…?" I said.

"We're going to *be* the snowballs," said Pan's dad.

"You're going to…? Sorry, what?" I asked.

But Min and Jayden seemed to have already caught on. As they started gathering up snow, I broke into a huge smile. The dragons' plan might just work!

Once we had a Mini-Dragon snowball each, Jayden pulled his sunglasses down from his head and placed them over his eyes. Then he took out two more pairs from his pocket and handed them to us.

"If we're going to do this, let's do it in style," he said.

"You carry spares?" asked Min.

"I got a couple of new pairs for Christmas," he said. "Besides, you can never have too many pairs of sunglasses."

I hoped he meant that, because he had another pair coming to him when he got my present.

"Come on, you chickens," shouted Grandad. "You have to come out some time."

"All right, on three," I whispered, putting on the shades. "One..."

"We promise we won't get you," sniggered Toby.

"Two..."

"Yeah, it's a ceasefire," laughed Mr Bloom. "Honestly."

"THREE!"

It felt like the world slowed down as we dived out from behind the shed, soaring across the garden as three white objects left our hands. As the ground fast approached,

we watched the snowballs fly up into the
air. There looked to be little chance of them
hitting Grandad and the Blooms, though,
and judging by their laughter the three of
them knew it.

WHACK!

WHACK!

Then three tiny pairs of wings popped out of the sides of the snowballs and suddenly they began to change direction, curving towards their intended targets. Only Grandad was smart enough to run, but the end result was the same.

CHAPTER 6

THERE BE DRAGONS

It was like a scene from a war film.
Grandad, Mr Bloom and Toby sprawled
out in the living room holding ice packs to
their heads and moaning loudly. The Mini-
Dragons had proven to be good snowballs.
Too good, if anything. After almost knocking
out their targets, Pan's parents had at least
had the good sense to grab their son and fly
back up through my window.

"I had hoped I might get a day off,"
laughed Jayden's mum. We were lucky she
was a nurse.

"Really, Eric," frowned Mum. "You could have taken it easier on your poor grandad."

Min, Jayden and I looked at each other, unable to believe what she was saying. Thankfully Gran was having none of it.

"Oh, don't blame them, Maya," she said. "They'll have had much worse, believe me. Doesn't know his own age, this one. He terrorizes our street whenever it snows."

"Where's Mum?" asked Toby, who was clutching his head like it might fall off.

"She's up in the spare room. On her phone, I think," said Jayden's dad.

"MUUUM!" shouted Toby, heading upstairs.

"D-d-dragon," muttered Grandad.

My face went white. So did Min's and Jayden's.

"What are you rabbiting on about now, George?" asked Gran.

"I saw it," he said slowly. "When it smacked into me. It was hiding in the snowball. It had tiny wings and a tiny beard … and it had glasses."

"You saw a tiny dragon with spectacles?" said Gran.

A wild-eyed Grandad nodded.

"George Crisp, I told you not to start on the sherry so early," scolded Gran. "Dragons with glasses indeed."

"Maybe it was the knock to the head?" suggested Mum.

But Grandad was undeterred. "You saw it, right, Frank?" he said, looking to Mr Bloom for support.

But Mr Bloom just laughed. "Dragons? Come on, George, give the kids their due. They got us good. Besides, everyone knows dragons aren't real. Now gremlins on the other hand…"

"What about you three?" said Grandad, turning to us.

"Er ... yeah, Grandad," I said. "You're right. We rolled three little dragons into snowballs and they used their wings to fly right into your heads."

Everyone burst out laughing, except for Grandad, who slumped into the couch, looking furious.

"Oh, don't get in a huff," said Gran, giving him a gentle nudge.

"Maybe I should go and see if Monty needs a hand with the dinner," he said.

"Don't you dare," warned Gran. "I'm sure he's got it all under control. Now why don't we play another board game?"

Grandad considered it for a few seconds, before mumbling something that sounded like, "OK then."

It was at that moment that I noticed three

tiny green heads bobbing past the living room.

"Sure, count me in. I'll be back in one second," I said, rushing out of the door. I caught them just before they reached the kitchen. I could hear Dad preparing dinner, singing along to Christmas songs on the radio.

"What are you doing?" I whispered. "What happened to staying in my room?"

"Being snowballs is hungry work," said Pan's dad. "We're starving."

"Can't you just have a few prawn crackers?" I said. "Pan's got some upstairs."

Pan nodded but his mum looked aghast. I knew she wasn't a massive fan of prawn crackers, even though they're one of the three main Mini-Dragon food groups, with dirty washing and goats being the others. I really hoped she didn't expect me to rustle up a goat for her.

"I thought you'd read the *Encyclopaedia Dragonica*?" she said. "Surely you know that when it comes to Christmas, Mini-Dragons and humans eat the same things? Turkey, stuffing, roast potatoes, gravy…"

"Those little sausages with the bacon round them," added Pan's dad, licking his snout.

"Right, fine, I'll get you something to eat. But you have to go back upstairs," I said. "Now!"

Pan's mum let out a long sigh. "Very well, if we must."

I scooped up the three of them and carefully made my way past the living-room door. Luckily everyone was too busy setting up a game of Word Battle to notice us.

But just as I reached the top of the stairs, I saw Toby walking into my room.

"Toby!" I said, quickly hiding the Mini-Dragons behind my back. "Where are you going?"

"To play with your stuff, obviously," said Toby.

"Er ... right," I said, trying to think of a way to get him out of there. "Hey, my new toys are all downstairs. Wouldn't you rather play with them?"

"Nah, your Christmas presents are rubbish," he said, grabbing a Slugwoman figurine and settling down on the floor. "I wish I had my presents. I asked Santa for three dragons. And I told him to make sure they were better than the one you've got, or those two defective ones you tried to pass off on me that time—"

"*Three* dragons?" I interrupted. "That does sound like fun. Well, I'll see you later, Toby." I started to close the door.

"You know," said Toby quickly. "If you wanted to cheer me up, you could let me play with that dragon toy of yours. Just so I can get some practice in…"

"Yeah, no chance," I said, shutting the door firmly. I put the dragons back down and pointed towards the spare room. "Quick, in here."

But as we stepped inside we froze.

Toby's mum was standing facing us. Well, facing her phone at any rate.

All that could be heard was the sound of her fingers tapping on the little screen. Her eyes were fixated on the device. Had she seen us? Did she even know we were there?

We appeared to get our answer a few seconds later when finally she frowned at her screen then walked out of the room, slamming the door behind her.

I almost collapsed with relief.

"Chatty, isn't she?" said Pan's dad.

Pulling myself together, I turned to the dragons. "I'll go and get you something to eat but you have to promise not to leave this room. Really, really promise this time."

The Mini-Dragons mumbled something.

"I need to hear it," I said.

"Dragon's honour," they said.

I left them and headed back downstairs. I was just stepping past the living room when an arm reached out and grabbed me. "There you are, Eric," said Grandad, pulling me inside. "It's a family Word Battle Royale – Crisps versus Blooms versus Lewises versus Songs. Ready to rumble?"

"Well, actually…" I said.

"Excellent," said Grandad. "Now maybe you can explain to Frank here that zoxyqoj is a perfectly good word."

"Use it in a sentence, then!" demanded Mr Bloom.

"Zoxyqoj," said Grandad. "As in, Frank's being a real zoxyqoj about this."

I was stuck there for the next hour and a half. Grandad wouldn't let anyone out of the room for fear they would head straight to the nearest dictionary. I couldn't help thinking that the words I was coming up with might have been slightly influenced by my upstairs guests:

HUNGRY DRAGONS BIG TROUBLE

It was only when an argument broke out after Grandad suspected Toby's mum had been looking up words on her phone (she had been, I saw her), that I was finally able to slip out.

Thinking about how annoyed Pan's parents were going to be with me, I almost didn't

hear the moaning coming from the kitchen.
But when I opened the door, there was Dad,
pacing the room and muttering to himself.

"Dad, what's wrong?" I asked.

"It's ruined, Eric... It's all ruined," he
groaned.

"What's ruined?" I asked.

"Christmas," said Dad, hanging his head.

"What are you talking about?" I said.

Dad pulled open the oven door. Inside
was a large, completely uncooked turkey.

CHAPTER 7
COLD TURKEY

"But didn't you put the oven on this morning?" I asked.

"I was going to," said Dad, slumping down at the kitchen table and holding his head in his hands. "I had just put the turkey in when the Blooms showed up. And then your grandparents. And then your friends."

"And you didn't notice it wasn't on?" I asked, suddenly realizing that the one thing missing from the house all day was that amazing smell of the Christmas turkey cooking. In my defence, I had been distracted with other things.

"I must have switched on the oven light but not turned on the heat," he said. "And then I was too busy preparing everything else and I used the bottom oven for that. All the trimmings are ready."

I looked at all the pots, filled with potatoes and vegetables. There was plenty of food but without the turkey it was shaping up to be a pretty lame Christmas dinner. "If you had to forget one thing," I said, "why couldn't it have been the sprouts?"

"Oh, your grandad is going to love this," said Dad glumly. "I honestly thought this was going to be the year I finally cooked the perfect dinner."

I patted him on the back. "Dad, if it's any consolation," I said, "I think Grandad will *always* be able to find something wrong with your cooking."

"You're probably right." Dad sighed.
"Well, I'd better go and break the news."

I followed Dad into the living room.

"Need any help, dear?" asked Mum.

"How's dinner coming along?" said
Grandad. "Hope you've not burned it like
last year?"

I felt so bad for Dad. If only there was a
way to cook a large turkey quickly.

I slapped my forehead. Of course!

"Where have you been?" said Pan as I burst into the spare room. The three Mini-Dragons were looking as grumpy as I'd expected.

"I'll explain later," I said. "But first I need your help."

"Why, what's wrong? Mum was about two minutes away from having a munch through your laundry basket, you know!" Pan laughed.

"I was not," Mrs Long snapped. "Now, where's the food you promised us?"

"That's the problem," I said. I explained about the turkey and my idea for how they could help. "So do you think you can do it?"

Pan's dad gave a little chuckle. "Do South American Swamp Dragons like to sunbathe?" he asked.

I looked at him blankly. "Er … I don't know."

Pan's dad sighed. "The answer is yes, Eric.

You really should read more of the *Encyclopaedia Dragonica* some time."

"I will," I said. "But can we go now? There's not much time."

Scooping up the Mini-Dragons I stuffed the three of them up the baggy sleeves of my Christmas jumper before heading back downstairs.

"How could you forget?" I heard Grandad say as we passed the living room. "There's undercooking but this is taking it to the extreme, son."

"Stop it, George," said Gran. "I'm sure Monty feels bad enough as it is..."

I closed the kitchen door behind us and shoved the wooden door wedge underneath it to make sure no one walked in on us.

I opened the oven and Pan peered inside. "Yep, definitely not cooked," he said.

"All right," said Mrs Long. "Eric, you'll

need to help."

"Me?" I asked. "But I can't—"

Pan's mum closed her eyes and rubbed her temple. "Yes, I'm well aware that you can't breathe fire. But we're going to need you to bring the turkey out of the oven."

My face turned pink, not that far off the colour of the turkey. "Oh, of course."

"When you do, you'll need to keep a hold of it," she said. "And you'll want to put on a pair of oven gloves."

"OK," I said, slipping on a pair of tartan oven gloves, before carefully pulling out the tray. It was much heavier than I'd expected and I had to steady myself for a moment.

"Right, Mini-Dragons, listen up," said Mrs Long, bringing Pan and Mr Long into a Mini-Dragon huddle. "I want a three-metre, full-power blast. Pan, you stand there. Cheng, you go there and I'll stand here so we have an equal flame distribution. Eric, in a second I'm going to need you to throw the turkey into the air. And then catch it. Everyone clear?"

The two Mini-Dragons nodded.

"Er … sorry. You want me to do what?" I said.

"Throw it in the air," she repeated casually, clearly confusing the giant turkey with a pancake. "Right, on three. One…"

"Yeah, it's just I'm not sure I can…"

"Two…"

"It's really heavy…"

"Three!"

With a massive grunt and using all my might, I somehow managed to toss the turkey in the air.

"Now!" shouted Pan's mum and three huge blasts of fire shot out of the dragons' mouths, blasting the turkey as it hovered above my head.

A second later, a fully cooked turkey landed back on the tray with a thud and miraculously I didn't drop it.

"You did it!" I said. But before I could thank them I heard voices getting closer. I covered the turkey with some tinfoil, shoved the tray back into the oven, switched it on and closed the door.

"Quick, out there," I said, pointing to the back door. The Mini-Dragons dived through the cat flap just as Grandad burst into the kitchen, followed by Dad and everyone else.

"Looks like it's up to me to save Christmas," said Grandad. "Don't worry, cooking for four hundred men every night in the army, you learn to improvise. Let me take a look."

It was too much for Dad. He turned away as Grandad opened the oven door, slipped on the oven gloves and slid out the tray.

"Is this some kind of joke?" said Grandad,
his face turning the colour of beetroot.

Gran obviously thought so, letting out
a huge belly laugh. Soon everyone but
Grandad was joining in.

Hearing the laughter, Dad finally turned
round.

"But … but … how?" he said.

"That was a bit mean of you, dear," said
Mum, trying her best to keep a straight face.

"Yes, very funny," said Grandad, shoving

the tray back in the oven, before storming out. "Let's all prank Grandad at Christmas."

"Nice one, Mr Crisp," said Jayden.

"Had me fooled," agreed Min.

"But … I was sure it wasn't cooked," said Dad to himself.

"Not another one at the sherry too early?" joked Gran.

Once everyone had left, Dad turned to me. "You saw it, didn't you? The turkey? I wasn't just imagining it, was I?"

I shrugged my shoulders. "I didn't really get a good look," I lied. "But it's not like it could have cooked itself, is it?"

Dad shook his head slowly. "I guess not," he said. "It has been a stressful day."

"Tell me about it," I muttered.

Dad pulled the tray out of the oven. "Wow, it really does look good, doesn't it?" he said.

"It looks great," I agreed. "In fact, it's going to be the best Christmas dinner ever."

Dad laughed. "Well, you might be getting a bit carried away there, Eric, but... Where are you off to?"

"Er ... toilet," I said as I rushed out of the room. The truth was, I finally knew what Pan could give his parents for Christmas.

CHAPTER 8

A MERRY LITTLE CHRISTMAS

"Can you guys come with me?" I whispered to Min and Jayden.

"But we just started playing," moaned Jayden, pointing towards the Who's the Murderer? game set up on the coffee table.

"Your gran suggested we play it to stop your grandad from whining," whispered Min.

I gave them a wild-eyed stare, the international sign for "Come on, we've got urgent Mini-Dragon business to deal with". Or at least it is in our world.

That was all they needed to see.

"Hey!" said Grandad as we hurried towards the door. "Where are you going?"

Min and Jayden looked at me.

My mind ran through possible excuses:

- Min and Jayden had to go home now. This might have worked on a normal day, when Min and Jayden's parents weren't in the same room.

- There was a fire in my bedroom. No, this would only cause bigger problems.

- We all just remembered we were allergic to board games. OK, this had more potential.

- We're nine years old, which is far too young to be leading murder investigations. Another possibility.

- We were going to help Dad set the table.

I plumped for the last one.

"Oh, that's very nice of you," said Mum.

"But they can't just leave without solving the murder," protested Grandad.

Jayden closed his eyes and rubbed his chin thoughtfully. "Was it Professor Partridge in the allotment, with the tea cosy?" he asked.

Grandad frowned as he picked up the sleeve in the middle of the board and pulled out the solution cards. "But … how did you know that?" he gasped.

"Elementary, my dear Eric's grandad," said Jayden, giving him a bow. "And now if you'll excuse us, we must be on our way."

At that moment, Toby reappeared, pushing past us into the living room.

"Oh, look, here's Toby," I said. "He can play the next game."

"Excellent," said Grandad, rubbing his hands together.

"Huh ... what?" said Toby as I shut the door behind me.

"How did you know that?" Min asked Jayden.

Jayden shrugged. "I've always been really good at intuition," he said. "Plus I saw the cards when Eric's gran was putting them in."

Min rolled her eyes, before turning to me. "So what do you need us for?" she asked.

"We're going to help Dad," I said.

"I thought you were just saying that to get us out of the room?" said Jayden.

"And I thought it was Pan who needed our help?" added Min.

"I was," I said. "And he does. But now that I think about it, helping Dad will let us help Pan." This didn't do much to get rid of the bewildered looks on their faces, so I told them my idea.

"Brilliant," said Jayden.

Min, on the other hand, seemed lost in thought. "I think I know how we can make this even better," she said. "You guys take care of things in there. I need to speak to your sister."

"Posy?" I said. "What for?"

"You'll see," she said with a smile. "Meet you upstairs in, what, ten minutes?"

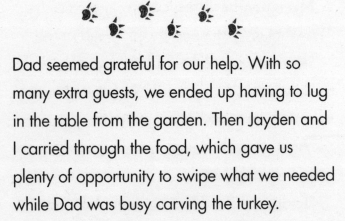

Dad seemed grateful for our help. With so many extra guests, we ended up having to lug in the table from the garden. Then Jayden and I carried through the food, which gave us plenty of opportunity to swipe what we needed while Dad was busy carving the turkey.

Once the table was set, we hurried upstairs to find Min waiting outside my door. Dad was already calling everyone for dinner so we didn't have much time.

"I thought the dragons were in the spare

room?" said Jayden.

"No, they're back in here," said Min. "I can hear them complaining about how hungry they are."

"They must have seen Toby heading downstairs when they flew back up from the kitchen," I said.

Jayden and Min looked at each other. "The kitchen?" they said together.

"I'll explain later," I said. I looked down at the tiny plates Min was holding from Posy's new tea set. "Good work, Min. They're just the right size. How did you convince her to give them to you?"

"I traded them for some chocolate from one of your selection boxes," she said. "I hope your parents won't mind."

I tried not to worry about that too much as Jayden and I emptied our pockets, filling the plates with little slices of turkey, stuffing,

Brussels sprouts, roast potatoes, pigs in blankets, carrots, turnip and parsnips, all snuck out of the kitchen under Dad's nose. I had even managed to carry out little egg cups full of gravy and cranberry sauce.

"All right, here we go," I said, pushing open the bedroom door.

"What's all this?" asked Pan's mum, looking up from a yoga book that had somehow managed to find its way into my room. I could tell from the way she quickly disentangled her legs from around her wings that she must have been in the middle of practising something from it.

"Merry Christmas, Mr and Mrs Long," I said, placing the tiny plates down in the middle of the room. Then I took out a can of lemonade I had stuffed up my jumper and tipped the contents into three little cups. "Pan thought it would be a nice idea for the three of you to have a proper Christmas dinner together."

"I did?" asked Pan. "Um... I mean, I did!"

"This is his present to you both," I said.

"Oh, wow, son!" said Pan's dad. "What a nice thing to do. Isn't that lovely, Isabel?"

But Pan's mum didn't reply. The bottom part of her snout trembled a little and then she burst into tears. She flung herself at Pan, squeezing him so hard that for a second I thought his head might pop off.

"This is wonderful," she sniffed.

"And you'll need these," said Min. She took out three tiny crackers from her pocket and handed them to the Mini-Dragons.

"Where did you get those from?" asked Jayden.

"Made them," she said. "We always make our own crackers. Posy had a brand-new craft set so I borrowed a few bits and pieces. Had to reduce the sizes obviously and make a few guesses on head sizes for the hats but..."

"You made hats as well?" I said.

Min gave me an odd look. "Of course I did. It wouldn't be Christmas without hats. It's not even worth thinking about."

Jayden nodded. "She's got a point, mate."

"Well, thank you all so much," said Pan's mum, once they'd pulled their mini-crackers and put on their hats.

"No problem, Mrs Long. We'd better go and get our own dinner now," I said. "So we'll leave you to it."

As we walked out, I saw Pan grinning at me. "Thanks," he mouthed.

I smiled and gave him a nod.

Suddenly Jayden turned on his heel. "Whoops, almost forgot," he said, reaching into his back pocket. He pulled out a dollop of red and white gloop and slapped it down on to a spare plate.

"It's trifle," he said. "Or at least I think it is. It's kind of hard to tell now. I'm sure it tastes fine, though."

"Er … yes, I'm sure it does," said Pan's mum, smiling politely.

We closed the door. With one Christmas meal sorted, it was time for another.

CHAPTER 9

THE LAWS OF CHRISTMAS

I had never known a Christmas dinner like it. Fifteen people and one cat crammed into a single room.

Seating was the biggest issue. The Blooms had nipped back home and brought over some chairs, which looked an awful lot like thrones to me, and Dad was using the office chair from the spare room. There were just enough seats for everyone. Well, if you can call the beanbag that I got stuck with a seat, that is.

Fifteen people having Christmas dinner

also meant fifteen crackers to pull, which
went like this:

BANG! BANG! BANG! BANG!

BANG! BANG! BANG! BANG!

BANG! BANG! BANG! BANG! BANG!

BANG! BANG! BANG! BANG! BANG

And then one extra for Pusskin:
BANG!

Mum always insists that Pusskin gets a hat
to wear, too. To be honest, I'm not sure she
appreciates it as much as Mum thinks she
does.

"All right, dig in," said Dad, placing the
turkey in the centre of the table. "I think there
should be enough for everyone."

That was an understatement. "I don't
understand, Dad," I said. "How can there still
be so much with all these people?"

"It's the first Law of Christmas," said Mr Bloom, helping himself to some gravy. "No matter how many people you invite to dinner, you'll always have too much food."

All the adults nodded in agreement. Dad had told me about the Laws of Christmas before:

- Christmas trees go up earlier every year.
- Time slows down the closer you get to Christmas, almost coming to a complete stop on Christmas Eve.
- Time corrects itself on Christmas Day, when it goes twice as fast.
- You will always get socks (although Dad says that when you get older, this changes to aftershave).
- Christmas TV is usually rubbish but no matter how hard you try, you'll still end up watching it.

Everyone tucked in. After a minute or two, all eyes turned towards Grandad, who had just placed a sliver of turkey into his mouth. The room fell silent, awaiting his verdict.

"Meh," he said eventually.

The look of disappointment on Dad's face was horrible to watch. But before anyone said another word, Gran snatched Grandad's plate and began shovelling his turkey back on to the serving plate.

"What are you doing?" cried Grandad.

"Well, if you don't like it, George, I'm sure Monty doesn't want you to force yourself to eat more," she said, throwing me a wink.

"All right, all right," Grandad said. "I didn't say I didn't like it. Fine. I'm sorry, son. You've outdone yourself this year. In fact, I think this might be the best Christmas dinner I've ever had. Maybe even better than the one I cooked back in '74 for five hundred men."

Dad seemed to get something caught in his eye for a minute. "Thanks, Dad," he said.

"It really is the Ultimate Christmas Dinner," said Mum, squeezing Dad's arm.

Gran smiled at Grandad, then returned the food to his plate.

"Though you've overcooked the Brussels sprouts," added Grandad.

"George!" protested Gran, taking a bite of one herself. After chewing it for a couple of seconds, her expression softened. "Actually, I'm sorry, but he's right there."

Dad let out a resigned laugh and the table fell silent as we all got stuck in again.

Just as Mum finished dishing out the trifle, there came a noise from across the table.

TING-TING!

Mrs Bloom had stood up and was tapping her wine glass.

"Oh-ho," said Mr Bloom, rubbing his

hands together. "Looks like Margery's going to give one of her famous toasts."

As the room fell silent, Mrs Bloom opened her mouth and...

BZZZZ. BZZZZ.

Her phone had lit up and was vibrating itself towards the end of the table. She held up her hand to everyone then hurried out to take the call.

"Ah, that's a shame," said Mr Bloom. "Well, I'd just like to thank the Crisps for taking us all in today and Monty for doing such a great job with the grub."

"Here, here," said Min's mum.

"Three cheers for the Crisps," said Jayden's dad.

HIP HIP, HOORAY!

HIP HIP, HOORAY!

HIP HIP, HOORAY!

Mr Bloom turned towards Toby, who was already tucking into his third portion of trifle. "What about you, Toby?" he said. "Is there anything you'd like to say?"

Toby's face, the bits that weren't covered in gravy and custard, turned red. "Erm … thanks," he mumbled.

"You're welcome, everyone," said Mum. "We've loved having you all here. Isn't that right, dear? Dear?"

But Dad was unlikely to reply, given that he was fast asleep in his chair, his head drooping into his pudding bowl.

"Anyone fancy helping me clean up?" said Mum. She was looking directly at me as she said this but fortunately there was no shortage of volunteers as Gran and Min's and Jayden's parents offered their services.

"Would you like to help, too, George?" asked Gran.

"I would, but I think my back's starting to play up," he said, rubbing the base of his spine.

I looked at Min and Jayden and tilted my head towards the door – our sign for "Let's quietly leave the room to go and check on the Mini-Dragons".

"Where are you off to, then?" asked Grandad. "Fancy another defeat ... I mean game of something?"

"Maybe later," I said. "We're just going to..."

"...go to Eric's room, to spend some time together before we go away," finished Min.

"What about your other friend?" Grandad asked, pointing at Toby.

"Well, he's not really..." started Jayden.

"...finished yet," I said.

Toby nodded and helped himself to the trifle from his mum's plate.

Ignoring the suspicious look on Grandad's face, the three of us left the room and hurried upstairs.

It seemed like the Mini-Dragons had enjoyed their Christmas dinner, too.

"Oh, man, that was amazing," said Pan, letting out a little flame belch.

"Yes, you must pass on our compliments to your father," said Mrs Long, patting her stomach. "I know we helped him out with the turkey but the rest of the meal was just divine. What is it he does for a living again? A chef, is he?"

"Actually, he's the manager of the most unsuccessful football team in the country," I said.

"Oh, yes, now I remember," she said. "Well, whatever makes him happy…"

Suddenly the door burst open and in stepped Grandad.

CHAPTER 10

I BELIEVE IN MINI-DRAGONS

"Ha!" cried Grandad, pointing his finger at each of the Mini-Dragons in turn. "Dragons! I knew it. They all thought I was off my rocker but I know what I saw."

Whenever they get frightened, Mini-Dragons automatically freeze themselves. According to the *Encyclopaedia Dragonica*, it's a defence mechanism. Min and Jayden appeared to be trying it out, too, as I looked to them for help. Maybe it was because I was so full of turkey, but I couldn't think of a single thing to say.

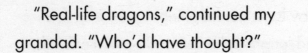

"Real-life dragons," continued my
grandad. "Who'd have thought?"

Laughter broke out behind Grandad.

I groaned. It was Toby, standing in the
doorway. As if things couldn't get any worse.

"What's so funny?" Grandad asked.

"You," said Toby. "You actually think
those things are real?"

Grandad looked at the dragons then back
to Toby. "Well … yes."

"First of all, everyone knows dragons are extinct," said Toby.

"That's dinosaurs," said Min, shaking her head.

"Whatever," said Toby. "Second, even if they were still alive, they wouldn't be that small, would they? And third, Eric's had one of those since his birthday. Do you honestly think in all that time, I wouldn't have been able to tell if it was a real dragon?"

Toby burst out laughing again. Min then started laughing herself and gave me a little nudge. I started laughing, too, as did Jayden.

Then Pan and his parents joined in.

"Not you three!" I hissed. Luckily neither Grandad nor Toby had noticed.

Grandad seemed to be thinking it over. "Yes, I suppose you would have to be a complete imbecile not to notice a real-life dragon under your nose all that time."

"Exactly!" agreed Toby.

"Well, what are they, then?" asked Grandad grumpily.

"They're toys, obviously," said Toby. "I tried for ages to get hold of one but you can't get them anywhere. Well, unless you're Eric. Look, there's another two he's got now. Unbelievable! Santa better have got me some or there's going to be trouble. And they'd better not be like those defective ones Eric tried to pass off on me. They kept complaining about the state of my room and telling me all about the history of dragons. Worst toys ever."

I could hear the muffled sounds of the Mini-Dragons giggling at his description of

Pan's horrible aunt and uncle.

Grandad still looked unconvinced. "Toys?" he said. "I saw them fly. And I'm pretty sure I heard them talking. What kind of toys do that?"

"I just told you they talk," said Toby, rolling his eyes. "And no offence but considering you've spent most of the day playing games that are like a hundred years old, I'm not sure you're that up to date when it comes to toys."

"I'm still up to date," Grandad said. "I bet I could beat you at any modern game you've got. What do you want to play? Hoopsies? Pins? Shuffles? Dusties?"

"Those don't even sound like real things," said Toby. "How about a proper game: Total Combat?"

"Er ... right," said Grandad, "I think I've heard of that board game."

Toby shook his head. "It's a video game."

"I knew that," said Grandad. "I meant *bored* game, in that I'm bored of playing it so much. And, actually, I've had a few sherries now so maybe I shouldn't…"

"No, that's perfect," grinned Toby. "Probably explains why you think you're seeing real dragons. Come on, I'll show you how it works."

"I know how it works," said Grandad.

"Sure you do," sighed Toby as they headed out of the room.

I shut the door behind them. We all stared at each other for a few moments before everyone erupted with laughter.

"Can I open my presents now?" asked Pan.

"Of course," said Mr Long. Pan's parents pulled their rucksacks out from beneath my bed and unzipped them, each removing a package wrapped in brown leaves. Mrs Long handed one to her son and Mr Long handed the other to me.

Pan sliced the leaf to shreds with his claws.

"It's a … stone," I said, looking at Pan's present.

"It's not a stone," laughed Isabel, even though it clearly was.

"It's my old bed," said Pan, smiling politely.

"Now you don't have to sleep in Eric's sock drawer every night," said Mr Long.

"Er … yeah, great," said Pan. I knew for a fact that he thought my sock drawer was the comfiest bed he'd ever had.

I opened my present to reveal another, pretty much identical, rock.

"Oh … a bed for me," I said.

Pan's parents looked bemused. "A bed?" said Mr Long. "How on earth are you going to fit on to that? Can't you tell the difference between a bed and a stone?"

"It's from our rock garden," said Pan's mum. "We thought you'd like it."

"Oh! It's … um … really nice," I said. "Thank you."

Mrs Long turned to Min and Jayden. "Sorry we didn't bring presents for you. We didn't really have room for anything else."

"That's OK," said Min.

"Yeah, don't worry about it," said Jayden.

It was time for Pan, Min, Jayden and me to exchange our gifts.

"That's a lot of prawn crackers," noted Pan's dad.

	ERIC	JAYDEN	MIN	PAN
ERIC GAVE TO		SUNGLASSES	BOOK VOUCHER	PRAWN CRACKERS
JAYDEN GAVE TO	SLUGWOMAN T-SHIRT		A FRAMED PICTURE OF MIN DRESSED AS EINSTEIN GIRL	PRAWN CRACKERS
MIN GAVE TO	CHOCOLATES	TOFFEES		PRAWN CRACKERS
PAN GAVE TO	PRAWN CRACKERS	PRAWN CRACKERS	PRAWN CRACKERS	

"The three of us chipped in to get you something else," I said, handing Pan another package. Beaming, he ripped it open.

"A scooter!" he said. "Just like yours."

That wasn't quite true. Pan's scooter was only about ten centimetres tall. It was designed for an action figure but was the ideal size for a Mini-Dragon.

"It's battery-powered," said Min.

"Yeah, according to the packaging it can reach speeds of up to one mile an hour," I added.

Pan and his dad grinned at each other.

"Oh, I think we can do better than that," said Mr Long.

CHAPTER 11
NAUGHTY AND NICE

The next day, Min, Jayden and Toby headed off for the airport. Toby emailed me once they had arrived in New York to tell me everything he had got. It was a long email.

Pan's parents stayed around until the new year, so Pan and I got to spend plenty of time with them. We managed to fit in quite a bit:

- pan's parents helped pan improve his flying. He's actually got a lot better, only crash-landing maybe one in five times now.

- Pan's dad made me read more of the Encyclopaedia Dragonica. There's actually a lot of interesting stuff in there. For example, did you know that dragons and giraffes don't get along? Me neither.
- Against my better judgement, we went to the cinema. It took some convincing for Mum to let me go "by myself". Pan was much better behaved than the last time — no food fights or anything. On the downside, Pan's parents insisted that we see a boring romantic film, then spent the entire time dragon-smooching

But eventually it was time for them to go. On the morning they were leaving, the snow had cleared a bit so Pan suggested we scoot out to Bramble Park to spend the last of our time together.

"Can't you stay a bit longer?" Pan asked his parents as we came to a stop in a secluded part of the park.

"We'd love to, son," said Pan's dad, "but if we don't get back soon, some other Mini-Dragons will have moved into our patch. The Zhang family have had their eyes on our rock garden for months."

"You could always come back with us," said Mrs Long. "I'd say you're a strong enough flyer now for mountain-living."

"It's your choice, of course," said Mr Long. "By Mini-Dragon laws, being able to fly means you can make your own decisions about things like that. But your mother and I would love to have you back home."

My heart sank. In all the chaos, it hadn't really occurred to me that Pan's parents might want to take him home with them. But before I could give the idea much thought, Pan was already shaking his head.

"No, I'm going to stay here," said Pan. "I think it's pretty obvious that Eric and his family need a Mini-Dragon around." Pan's parents quickly nodded in agreement. "But maybe I can come and visit soon?" he added.

"That would be lovely," said Pan's mum, wiping a tear from her eye, before giving Pan a massive squeeze. Then she turned and gave my wrist a hug.

"And you're welcome to stay again," I said. "Though if you can call ahead next time..."

Pan's dad shook my pinkie finger. "Perhaps we'll come back next year," he said. "And it's a leap year ... you know what that means?"

I did. In the Dragonian Calendar, the extra day in a leap year gets added to December 25th, making...

"DOUBLE CHRISTMAS!" shouted Pan in delight.

Given how hectic one Christmas with the Longs had been, I tried not to think about what a two-day event would be like.

"Sorry you couldn't meet my mum," I said to Mrs Long. "I know how much you were looking forward to it. I just don't think it would have been a good idea."

"Er ... yes, not a problem." Mrs Long's eyes suddenly started darting back and forth. "Ahem ... I suppose we should be off, then..."

She swung round to grab her backpack but accidentally knocked it over with her tail. A glossy sheet of paper tumbled out of it.

"What's this?" I said, picking it up.

"NOTHING, IT'S NOTHING!" she shouted.

I held up the paper to reveal a picture of Mrs Long giving the thumbs up to the camera. Behind her was my sleeping mum, drooling away on her pillow.

"Wait a minute … you snuck into my parents' bedroom?" I asked. "When—"

Pan's mum snatched the photo out of my
hand. "OK, got to go," she said, planting a
final kiss on Pan's forehead, before shooting
off into the sky. "TALK SOON!"

Pan's dad shrugged. "Nothing to do
with me," he said, before launching himself
after her.

Pan and I watched them in silence until they had disappeared into the clear blue sky.

"Hang on ... so who took that photo, then?" I said. "And who printed that picture for her?"

But Pan wasn't there. I looked round just in time to see a tiny scooter zipping off into the distance.

"Pan, come back!" I shouted, jumping on to my own scooter. "PAN!"

Find out about how Pan came to live with Eric in...

CHAPTER 1
A CHANGE OF FORTUNE

"Hey, Eric," said the tiny short-haired girl standing outside my front door. Min Song and I were in the same class at school, but right now she was here on official business, which was why she was carrying a dozen Chinese takeaway boxes under her chin. "Sorry we're so late."

"Er ... we ordered five minutes ago," I said, checking my watch.

"I know, I know, but traffic was a nightmare," she said, nodding towards her dad who was sitting on a moped with the words "Panda Cottage" emblazoned on the side, impatiently tapping his watch.

"No, what I meant was—" But before I could finish Min had shoved the huge pile of boxes into my arms.

Then she picked up a box that had fallen to the ground. "Oh, and don't forget your beansprouts."

"Beansprouts?" I said, looking puzzled. "I don't think we ordered—"

"No, they're free," interrupted Min. "We have way too many of them. Please, just take it."

"Oh, OK," I said. "You know, I've never actually tried them."

"You'll love them. Probably. Anyway, I have to go."

I put down the boxes and handed her the money, before she hopped on the moped and it disappeared down the road.

"Min took her time!"

That's my dad, Monty Crisp. He's the reason we were having a Friday-night Chinese. My dad manages the local football team, the Kippers, and we were celebrating their latest success – a 10–1 scoreline.

"I still can't believe it," he said as I handed him the boxes. "We got an actual goal. First time in five years. All right, so technically it was the other team that scored it for us, but an own goal still counts!"

Sorry, I should have been more clear: They *lost* 10–1.

The Kippers are the worst football team of all time. In their fifty-year history they've only ever won a single game, and even then it was because the other team had to forfeit after getting stuck in traffic.

"You should be very proud, dear," said my mum, Maya. In case you're wondering, her legs are currently over her head because she's a yoga instructor, not because she's weird. Though she is weird.

Mum unfolded herself and joined me,
Dad, my two-and-a-half-year-old sister Posy
and our horrible, definitely evil, cat Pusskin
at the kitchen table.

Half an hour later, the Crisp family was
officially stuffed, as you can see from my
helpful diagram:

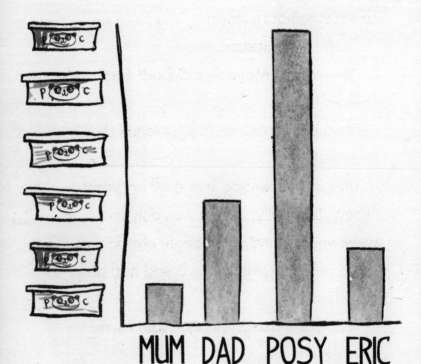

MUM DAD POSY ERIC

The number of boxes for Posy is misleading. Those are the number of *actual boxes* she attempted to eat. She doesn't bother about the food, she just loves chewing plastic.

After dinner, Dad was back talking sport.

"All I'm saying, Eric," he said, reaching for the fortune cookies, "is that it wouldn't kill you to take an interest in athletic pursuits. Like football or rugby or..."

"Yoga?" suggested Mum.

"Be serious, Maya," said Dad. "Er... I mean..."

Mum glared at him. "I'll pretend I didn't hear that."

Dad mimed wiping sweat off his brow. "Phew. But really, Eric, it was only last week you told me you thought offside was when only *one* side of the bread had gone mouldy..."

"He was *teasing*, Monty," said Mum.

"You *were* teasing him, weren't you, Eric?"

Before I could reply Dad cut in: "Hey, would you look at that?"

He held up a small piece of paper.

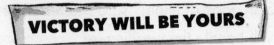

VICTORY WILL BE YOURS

"You beauty!" cried Dad. "It's destiny."

I rolled my eyes. "Everyone knows fortune cookies are rubbish, Dad. The last one I got said 'Your shoes will make you happy'."

"And did they?" Dad asked.

"Not that I noticed..."

"What did you get this time, Eric?" asked Mum.

I cracked open the shell and unfurled the piece of paper inside.

YOUR LIFE IS ABOUT TO CHANGE

"Hmm. Well, you do turn nine soon," Mum said.

"A week tomorrow," I reminded her. She *probably* knew that already but my birthday was WAY too important to take any chances with.

"Ooh, look at mine," said Mum. "'Your son will handle the washing-up'."

"It doesn't say that," I said.

"Well, all right," she admitted. "It's actually the same as Dad's."

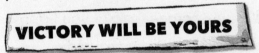

VICTORY WILL BE YOURS

"But you cleaning up will be a nice victory for me," she said.

I let out a groan but I knew from experience that I had about as much chance of getting out of it as the Kippers did of winning, well ... anything.

I rinsed out all the boxes and took them outside. I'd almost finished putting them in the recycling bin when I realized that the box of beansprouts was still unopened.

Even though I was stuffed, I was curious to find out what they tasted like. I opened the lid and jumped back in fright. Not because of the beansprouts, though they didn't look that appetizing, but because nestled inside the box was a small green scaly object. It had:

A long dragon-like snout.

A long dragon-like tail.

Big dragon-like wings.

Sharp dragon-like teeth.

Short dragon-like arms and legs.

Dragon-like claws.

There was no doubt about it. Whatever it was looked a lot like a dragon. Its tiny marble-like black eyes seemed to stare back at me and, for the briefest of moments, I almost convinced myself it was real.

Ha. A real dragon. Can you imagine?

Were Panda Cottage giving out free toys
with their food now?

"Snappy Meals," I said out loud, before
remembering there was no one around to
laugh at my joke.

I took the toy out of the box and was
surprised by how it felt. Whatever it was
made of, it wasn't plastic. I once touched

a lizard at the zoo and it felt quite similar
– rough and cool to the touch – but this
was much, much harder. It really was
the most lifelike toy I had ever seen. It
must have taken forever to paint. Not
that it even looked or felt painted, mind
you. It was too realistic. Every scale was
a different shade of green, with small,
freckle-like flecks of yellow across the
snout. Gently, I moved its arms and legs
back and forth, feeling a little resistance
as I did so, almost as if it didn't appreciate
me doing it.

Whoever had made it must have gone to
some trouble – way more than a free Chinese
takeaway toy was worth, that's for sure.

After trying a handful of beansprouts and
deciding I wasn't a fan, I shoved the dragon
into my pocket, went back inside and headed
upstairs. After all, it was Friday and I had a

lot to do. My comics weren't going to read
themselves.

I put the tiny dragon on a shelf before
diving on to my bed and settling into issue
#437 of my favourite comic: *Slugman*.

A short while later, Slugman was
just about to take a call from the Police
Commissioner on the Slug Phone when I felt
something tugging at my trouser leg.

"Yeah?" I said, too absorbed in the story
to bother looking down.

"What you reading?" said a childish voice.

"Oh, it's the latest issue of *Slugman*," I
replied.

"Any good?" asked the voice, which
sounded like it had a Chinese accent.

"It's amazing," I said. "He's about to fight
his arch-enemy, The Salt Shaker."

"Cool. I love comics. I mean, I haven't
actually *read* any, but they look awesome."

"Help yourself," I said, still not taking my eyes off the page but pointing towards the pile at the side of my bed.

"Don't mind if I do. Thanks!"

"No worries," I said.

I continued to read for a few seconds more, before it finally dawned on me. Slowly, I lowered the comic and looked towards the end of my bed.

Sitting there, reading a *Captain Bin-Man* comic with his dragon-like claws, was the dragon toy from the beansprout box.

YOUR LIFE IS ABOUT TO CHANGE

Two things were clear to me:

The toy dragon was not a toy.

Whoever makes Panda Cottage's fortune cookies had really raised their game this time.

COLLECT THE WHOLE SERIES!

Eric agrees to take Pan to school with him – and quickly regrets it!

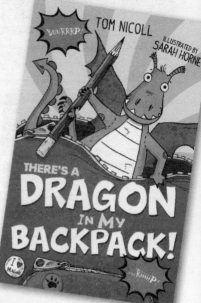

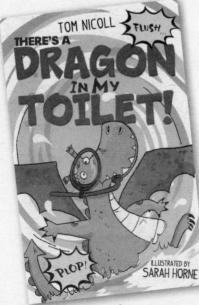

Pan's relatives come to visit ... via the sewers!

Eric and Pan go camping. What could possibly go wrong?

Eric and Pan enter a film competition. But Toby has Hollywood dreams, too…

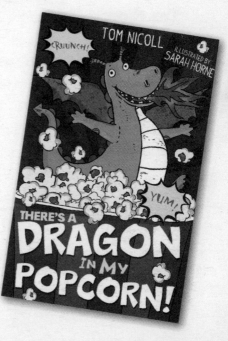

ABOUT THE AUTHOR

Tom Nicoll has been writing since he was at school, where he enjoyed trying to fit in as much silliness to his essays as he could possibly get away with. When not writing, he enjoys playing video games (especially the ones where he gets beaten by kids half his age from all over the world). He is also the author of BOYBAND OF THE APOCALYPSE. There are no dragons in that.

Tom lives just outside Edinburgh with his wife, daughter and a cat that thinks it's a dog.

ABOUT THE ILLUSTRATOR

Sarah Horne grew up in Derbyshire and spent much
of her childhood scampering in the nearby fields with
a few goats. Then she decided to be sensible and
studied Illustration at Falmouth College of Arts and
gained a Master's degree at Kingston University.

She now lives in London and
specializes in funny, inky illustration.

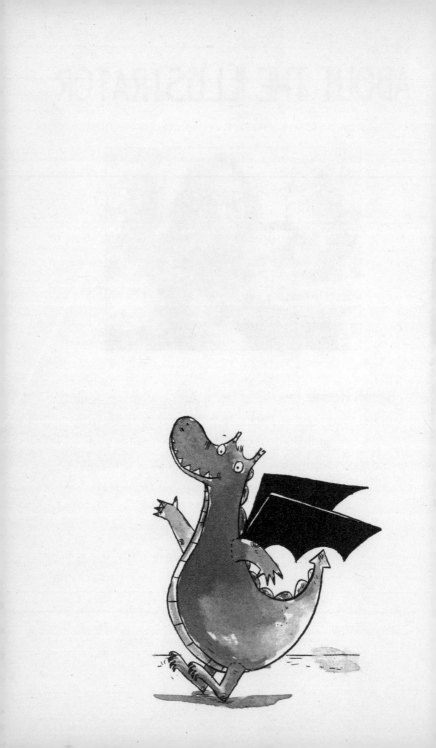